Happy

Love, Granny & Grandpa
april 11, 2008

DIANE SWANSON

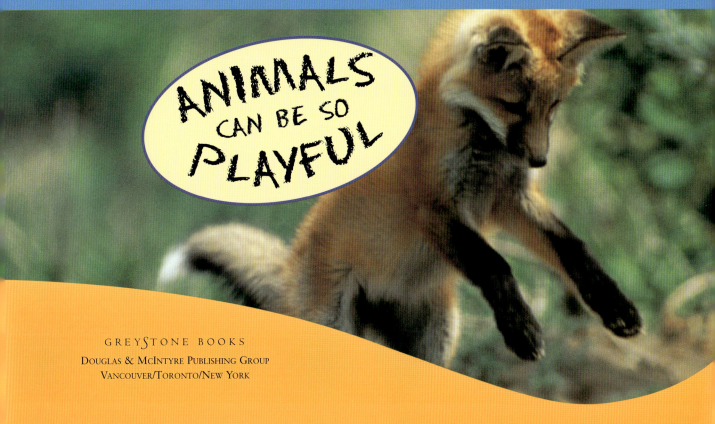

ANIMALS CAN BE SO PLAYFUL

GREYSTONE BOOKS
DOUGLAS & MCINTYRE PUBLISHING GROUP
VANCOUVER/TORONTO/NEW YORK

CONTENTS

Swinging,

Rolling,

Diving,

Animals can be so playful.

I SPY, YOU SPY
Find who's swinging,
who's rolling, who's diving.

1

...pouncing.....

Run! Spring!

A red fox pup is pouncing.

When it plops down on its brother,

The real fun begins.

I SPY, YOU SPY

Find how a fox holds its tail as it pounces.

...swinging.....

Deep in the jungle,

An orangutan sw-i-ngs.

It grabs leafy branches

And swoops—tree to tree.

I SPY, YOU SPY

Find which are longer—the orangutan's legs or its arms.

jumping

6

Free of the sea,

The dolphins are jumping.

With high leaps and tail flips,

They sail through the air.

I SPY, YOU SPY

Find the trails of water the dolphins are making.

7

...romping...

Cub on cub,

Two frisky lions romp.

First one's on top, then the other,

Trading nip for nip.

I SPY, YOU SPY

Find the tongue on the cub being nibbled. It's sticking out in pleasure.

...wrestling....

Grab a partner, twirl around.
Prairie dogs are wrestling.
The sun is out and so are they,
Chasing, snatching, tumbling.

I SPY, YOU SPY

Find the ever-wagging
tail of a prairie dog.

11

...**rolling**...

12

Toes on nose

And front paws tucked in tight,

A polar bear rolls in a ball—

A snowy ball of fur.

I SPY, YOU SPY

Find the snow that's clinging
to the polar bear's coat.

13

...leaping.......

Hippity hop, a lemur (LEE-mur) leaps.

Its arms fly by its sides.

With a balancing tail and long, strong legs,

It bounces down the trail.

I SPY, YOU SPY

Find the thick padding on the bottom of the lemur's foot.

...diving......

Dashing, darting, diving,
Zooming all about,
A gang of husky sea lions
Clowns around together.

I SPY, YOU SPY

Find which sea lion
is diving the deepest.

...hanging out...

Three furry raccoons

Are hanging out together.

Two are swinging front to back,

And—oops!—one's slipping sideways.

I SPY, YOU SPY

Find the long toes and sharp claws that help raccoons grip.

Swinging,
Rolling,
Diving,
Animals can be so

playful.

Points for Parents

Red foxes are wild dogs that have red, gray-brown, or silvery black coats. They're adaptable enough to live almost everywhere—except deserts and dense woods.

Polar bears are huge mammals that live on islands and along coasts in countries around the Arctic Ocean.

Orangutans are great apes—not monkeys—that swing through jungles in Borneo and Sumatra. Their name means "man of the woods" in the Malay language.

Lemurs are primates—the mammal order that includes humans and orangutans—and are found mostly in forests in Madagascar and its neighboring islands.

Bottlenose dolphins are small toothed whales with beaklike snouts. Look for them along coasts of the Atlantic Ocean.

Sea lions are eared seals, marine mammals that often swim in cold seas. They're clumsy on land but graceful in water.

Lions are Earth's largest cats. You'll find them in the grasslands of Africa and a small part of India.

Common raccoons are native to North and Central America. They're especially at home in wooded areas close to water. Some spend their whole lives in cities.

Black-tailed prairie dogs are rodents in the squirrel family. They form large colonies in underground burrows on the prairies of North America.

Greystone Books
A division of Douglas & McIntyre Ltd.
2323 Quebec Street, Suite 201
Vancouver, British Columbia V5T 4S7
www.greystonebooks.com

National Library Cataloguing in Publication Data

Swanson, Diane, 1944-
    Animals can be so playful

    ISBN 1-55054-900-6 (bound).—ISBN 1-55054-904-9 (pbk.)
    1. Play behavior in animals—Juvenile literature. I. Title.
QL763.5.S92 2002   j591.5   C2002-911029-4

Library of Congress Cataloging information is available.

Packaged by House of Words for Greystone Books
Editing by Elizabeth McLean
Cover and interior design by Rose Cowles
Cover photograph by J. D. Cox/First Light
Photo credits: p. i J. D. Cox/First Light; p. ii (clockwise from top) Mattias Klum/First Light, David Doubilet/First Light, First
Light; p. 2 J. D. Cox/First Light; p. 4 Mattias Klum/First Light; p. 6 S. Westmorland/First Light; p. 8 Beverly Joubert/First Light;
p. 10 Raymond Gehman/First Light; p. 12 First Light; p. 14 E. Robert/First Light; p. 16 David Doubilet/First Light;
p. 18 Thomas Kitchin/First Light

Printed and bound in Hong Kong

A very special note of thanks goes to Dr. Alison Preece, Faculty of Education, University of Victoria, for her guidance
and encouragement in the development of this series.

The publisher gratefully acknowledges the support of the Canada Council for the Arts and of the British Columbia Ministry
of Tourism, Small Business and Culture. The publisher also acknowledges the financial support of the Government of Canada
through the Book Publishing Industry Development Program (BPIDP).